GREAT HIT!

Rob Childs

Illustrated by Michael Reid

Also available:
GREAT SAVE!
GREAT SHOT!

For My Great Mum!

GREAT HIT!
A CORGI PUPS BOOK: 0 552 54637 2

First publication in Great Britain

PRINTING HISTORY
Corgi Pups edition published 2000

1 3 5 7 9 10 8 6 4 2

Set in 18/25 pt Bembo Schoolbook

Corgi Books are published by Transworld Publishers,
61–63 Uxbridge Road, London W5 5SA,
a division of The Random House Group Ltd,
in Australia by Random House Australia (Pty) Ltd,
20 Alfred Street, Milsons Point, Sydney, NSW 2061, Australia,
in New Zealand by Random House New Zealand Ltd,
18 Poland Road, Glenfield, Auckland 10, New Zealand
and in South Africa by Random House (Pty) Ltd,
Endulini, 5A Jubilee Road, Parktown 2193, South Africa

Made and printed in Great Britain by
Cox & Wyman Ltd, Reading, Berkshire

Contents

Series Reading Consultant: Prue Goodwin,
Reading and Language Information Centre,
University of Reading

Chapter One

"Brill!" cried Tom, the team captain. "Best goal of the match."

Tom wrapped his arm round the scorer's slim shoulders. "Don't know how you put so much bend on the ball," he grinned.

"Nor do I," Rebecca admitted. "I just hit it."

The beaten goalkeeper booted the ball away in disgust. He

thought he'd had the shot well covered until the ball swerved out of his reach.

"No idea what the score is now," he muttered. "I've lost count."

The score was even worse
than his maths. Rebecca's second
goal had put Great Catesby 9–2
ahead. The Greats were living
up to the name on the back of
their red shirts.

"We want ten!" chanted the
home fans. "We want ten!"

"C'mon, men," shouted Tom, ignoring the fact that there were two girls in the team of six. "There's still enough time to make it double figures."

The first of the Greats to touch the ball again, however, was goalkeeper Hannah – and that was only to pick it out of the tangled netting. The long-range shot had taken her by surprise and the ball skidded underneath her diving body.

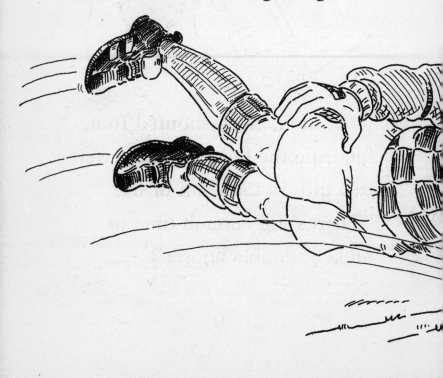

The captain was not best pleased. "That was sloppy, men!" Tom moaned. "C'mon, concentrate! The game's not over till the final whistle."

A minute later, it ended in the same way as it had begun – with another goal by top-scorer Jonty.

The keeper dived to his right to make a good save, but he couldn't hold on to the ball. Jonty pounced on the rebound, stretching out a leg to poke the ball into the net.

"Goal!" he cried. "That's my fourth!"

"And it's also number thirteen in the match," said Tom, ruffling Jonty's ginger hair in delight. "Unlucky for some."

"Huh!" grunted the keeper. "More unlucky for me than you, I'd say."

★

"Ten-three!" exclaimed Michael
in the boys' cloakroom afterwards. "That's got to be some
kind of record."

"I'm more interested in the record we're making tomorrow," said Imran, Michael's partner in defence. "Hey, Jonty-boy! What time's your dad wanting us in the morning?"

Jonty reddened. He didn't like anybody but his dad calling him by that name.

"About ten o'clock," he replied. "You know that."

"Yeah, I was just wondering whether he'll be up by then," Imran laughed. "I didn't think pop stars got out of bed till the afternoon!"

Jonty's dad was better known as the Red Fox. The famous singer had recently moved into Great Catesby and he was going to record a special song with the children. Everyone hoped it would raise enough money to help save the little village school from being closed.

Tom started to chant the song's chorus and the others quickly joined in, their voices bouncing off the walls.

"C'mon, you Greats! C'mon you Greats!
Come and watch us win our games,
Come and shout out all our names.
C'mon, you Greats! C'mon you Greats!"

"Cor! It doesn't half echo around in here!" laughed Michael.

"It'll sound much better
tomorrow," said Jonty.

"Bound to, y'know, in a
proper recording studio like your
dad's had built at the Manor,"
Tom pointed out.

"I didn't mean that," Jonty grinned. "I meant the girls will be with us then – and they can sing much better than you noisy lot!"

Chapter Two

The next morning, Mrs Roberts
led the footballers and members
of the school choir through the
village towards the Manor.

"Keep up at the back there," the teacher called out towards Imran's group of stragglers. "We don't want to be late."

"Won't matter," he said. "Bet the Red Fox won't even be up yet."

Michael chuckled. "Perhaps the studio's in his bedroom!"

The jokers were in for a surprise. The Red Fox himself greeted the party at the iron gates of the old Manor – fully dressed – before showing them towards a low, modern building in the grounds.

"Magic!" breathed Rebecca, a
big fan of the Red Fox, as she
stepped inside and gazed around
the studio in wonder. "This is
like a dream come true. It's just
too incredible for words."

"I hope not," hissed Tom. "Cos we've now got to start singing them!"

They listened first to the music that had already been recorded by the Red Fox's own band, the Earthlings.

"So what do you reckon?" he asked.

"Brill!"

"Magic!"

"Great!"

"It's perfect!" smiled Mrs Roberts. "Thanks so much."

"No trouble, lovely lady," replied the Red Fox, making everyone laugh at the way he spoke to their teacher. "Let's just hope it does the trick."

"Course it will," said Jonty confidently. "So now let's get the words on that tape as well, Dad, OK?"

"OK, you're the boss!" grinned the Red Fox, breaking into song.

"*It's great, boy, it's great,*
Feeling part of a team."

The pop star and his son then formed a duet to sing the rest of the first verse.

"*Playing towards the same goal,*
Working together —
sharing a dream."

As arranged, the Red Fox
sang the second verse with
Rebecca as his partner. She was
feeling so nervous, her voice
sounded a little squeaky, but it
didn't matter. This was only a
practice.

"It's great, girl, it's great,
Being on the same side.
Whether we win, lose or draw,
Whatever the score – knowing we
tried."

Everyone joined in the chorus
and then the pattern was
repeated with the next two
verses. This time, though, the
Red Fox sang along with all the
boys, followed by all the girls.

It took the rest of the day to rehearse and get everything right, stopping only for a short picnic lunch outside in the autumn sunshine.

"Phew!" breathed Imran, chewing on a sandwich. "Didn't know making a record could be such hard work."

"Practice makes perfect," said Tom. "Just like with soccer. You have to try and make all that work in training pay off in a real match."

Chapter Three

The Greats' next practice turned
out to be rather different than
normal. They were performing
their soccer skills in front of lots
of cameras to gain extra publicity
for their fund-raising.

The Fox Cubs, as the record company called them, were not only going to appear on the CD case, but also have their pictures in the newspapers and on local television!

The Red Fox joined in the practice, too, but he was clearly a much better singer than a footballer. He kept tripping up over the ball and his snazzy tracksuit was soon covered in mud.

"Hope they don't put that one
of me in the papers," he laughed
as the photographers snapped
him missing an open goal.

"Never mind, Dad, you can't be a star at everything," grinned Jonty.

"You will be, Jonty-boy – that's for sure," said the Red Fox, slapping his son on the back. "On and off the pitch."

All the fuss that the Greats were receiving did not go down too well with some people. Tom's cousin Jack, who lived in the nearby town of Kilthorpe, was green with envy when he saw the Greats playing football on television.

"You lot looked rubbish!" Jack scoffed when the Curtis family had a weekend get-together soon afterwards. "And you can't even sing."

Tom laughed it off. "You're just jealous!"

"Rubbish!" snorted Jack, using his favourite word again. "The Red Fox should've come to our school if he wanted to film some decent footballers. We could thrash you lot any day."

"No chance!"
"Oh, yeah?"
"Yeah!"
"Right," Jack decided. "Guess we'll just have to prove it, then . . ."

First thing on Monday morning, the cousins both asked their teachers if a challenge match could be arranged between the two schools. Only neither of them put it quite like that. Tom called it a 'friendly'.

"An excellent idea!" beamed
Mrs Roberts. "If the worst comes
to the worst and our school does
have to close, at least you will
have had the chance to meet
some of your future classmates."

Mr Savage, the Kilthorpe Primary sports teacher, thought it was a good idea too, but he insisted on playing eleven-a-side.

This caused Mrs Roberts a couple of problems. Firstly, she wasn't sure if there were as many as eleven children in her small class who were really up to standard. And secondly, they didn't have that many shirts.

A fortnight later, after several extra practice sessions, the Greats did manage to raise a full team – just – but only by including the Berry twins, Stephen and Rachel (or Strawberry and Raspberry, as they were better known). What the twins lacked in footballing ability, they made up for in stamina. They could both keep running all day.

Mr Savage solved the other snag by digging out some tatty, reddish tops from his own school's P.E. store for the five extra players to wear.

Sadly, the game did not start well for the Greats. Not used to playing on such a big pitch, their defence had almost as many holes in it as Strawberry's shirt.

Hannah came to her team's rescue in the very first minute, making a fine save right on the goal-line.

But the keeper had no chance with the next shot. The ball struck Michael's shoulder and looped up into the top corner of the net well out of her reach.

"Wish I'd known how good Jack's lot were," Tom muttered as another shot clunked against Hannah's post. "This could get very embarrassing."

Chapter Four

The Greats had Hannah to
thank for only being 3–0 down
at half-time. It was a good job
their overworked goalkeeper was
on top form or the score would
have been much worse.

Tom glared at Strawberry. "Might help if some of us didn't keep giving the ball away to the other team," he moaned during the break.

"Not my fault," Strawberry said hotly. "It's this stupid shirt they gave me. Seems to think it's still on their side."

"Best excuse I've ever heard," giggled Imran. "A haunted shirt!"

He didn't find it so funny when Strawberry went and scored at the start of the second half – in his own goal.

Taking a huge swing at the ball, Strawberry some-how sliced it over his head to send it spinning into the net.

Jack mocked his cousin. "You lot are rubbish!" he taunted. "Our goalie hasn't even got his knees dirty yet."

"Plenty of time left yet to make him need a bath," Tom retorted.

"Good joke, Tom," Jack sniggered, trotting away.

"C'mon, men!"
Tom cried, shaking
his fists at his
teammates.
"Let's show
'em how we
can really play."

It was almost as if Tom had
waved a magic wand instead.

The Greats went straight up
the other end and hit back with
a surprise goal.

Raspberry and Rebecca linked up well along the wing and created a shooting chance for Jonty. He fired the ball low and hard towards the target and it slithered wide of the goalkeeper's dive into the corner of the net.

The Greats were too busy celebrating to notice how muddy the goalie's knees were now when he stood up.

Unfortunately, Jonty's effort was not to spark off any fairy-tale revival. That tends to happen only in storybooks.

The two cousins soon knew
that they weren't imagining
things when they jumped for the
ball together and clashed heads
in mid-air. The pain was too
real for it to be make-believe.

"You've got a hard nut," Tom
said, gently touching the lump
on his forehead. "Felt like I'd
been hit by a cannonball!"

Dazed, Tom and Jack were led off the pitch to recover on the touchline. The Greats didn't have the luxury of a substitute so they were now 4–1 behind and also a player short.

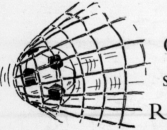 To their credit, the Greats did score a second goal when Rebecca netted from close range, but they couldn't prevent Kilthorpe increasing their total. The Killers, as they were nicknamed, shot a fifth past Hannah and then added another in injury time to make it six.

"Easy! Easy!" Jack taunted his cousin after the final whistle. "The Killers murdered you!"

"We'll play you again next term when we've had a bit more practice at this eleven-a-side lark," said Tom. "Then we'll see who comes out on top."

"Huh!" Jack snorted. "You've got as much chance of doing that as your rubbish song has of being top of the pops!"

As the players trudged off the pitch, a phone was heard ringing and Jonty scurried over to pick up his coat from near the touch-line. To everyone's amazement, he pulled out a mobile phone and put it to his ear.

"We're a hit!" he shrieked, waving the phone about in the air. "We're at number six!"

"What yer talking about?" Michael muttered. "More like we've just been hit for six."

"Dad's just told me we're in the charts," Jonty cried. "*C'mon, you Greats!* has gone straight in at number six!"

His teammates could hardly believe such amazing news at first, but then burst into the song's chorus.

C'mon, you Greats! C'mon, you Greats!
Come and watch us win our games."

The Killers began to jeer and the singing came to a halt.

"Never mind them," said Mrs Roberts. "Just remember how the second verse goes."

The two goalscorers, Jonty and Rebecca, picked up the teacher's cue and began a little duet.

"Whether we win, lose or draw, Whatever the score, knowing we tried."

Jack smirked at his cousin. "Seems like you'll have to try a

bit harder in future. The score was
six-two, remember."

Tom pretended to look puzzled.
"Sorry, don't remember that.
Must be that bang on the bonce I
had," he grinned.

"Well you still lost!" Jack insisted.

"So what?" said Tom with a shrug. "It'll just make us even more determined to beat you next time. We aim to be the best – the number one!"

THE END